I dedicate this book to my boys. I love you for the way you love
and care for your sister, BUT most of all, I love you for being you.
You're funny, smart, adventurous, and have the kindest hearts of anyone I know.
You are both so amazing, and I am so proud to be your mom.

To my husband Toby, who always believes and never stops encouraging.

To Maya, you were born with an indomitable spirit, never forget it.

Bee Mighty Press
Mightymissmaya.org
Text and illustration copyright © 2020 by Bee Mighty Press
First Edition

ISBN 978-1-7357386-0-4

*Bee Mighty Press provides special discounts when purchased in larger volumes
for premiums and promotional purposes, as well as for fundraising and educational use.
Custom editions can also be created for special purposes. For information on speaking engagements,
school visits, and other special requests please visit our website mightymissmaya.org.*

MIGHTY MISS MAYA

SEE IT, THEN BE IT

by Ann Tisdale

Illustrations by Daniel Włodarski

I'm Maya. This is Abby, my Goldendoodle.
She is the sweetest dog, part retriever, part poodle.

Abby is different, just like me.
She doesn't have four paws; she only has three.

We're going on adventures daring and grand.
We might climb tall mountains or play in the sand.
I hope we see leopards and otters that dance.
Adventures await if we just take a chance!

"You're too small for adventures,"
some grown-ups will say.
But that won't get me down
or stand in my way.

"See it, then be it," I say each day.
If I believe I CAN, I'm nearly halfway.

Mom said I was born just knowing I CAN.
Here is the story of how it began.
I was born very early and really quite small.
Right from the start, I had to give it my all.

"She's tiny but mighty," the nurses would say.
"She's one fierce girl, and she grows stronger each day."
"You're mighty," my mom and dad whispered to me.
"Mighty Miss Maya, you were born to be."

Mighty Miss Maya, a nickname that stuck.
I'm a kid with a plan and a whole lot of pluck.

Enough with all that,
I don't want to run out of time.
I see a big mountain I know I can climb.
High in the mountains, who knows what I'll see.
Was that a moose flying by on one ski?

"See it, then be it," I always say.
If I believe I can, I'm nearly halfway.

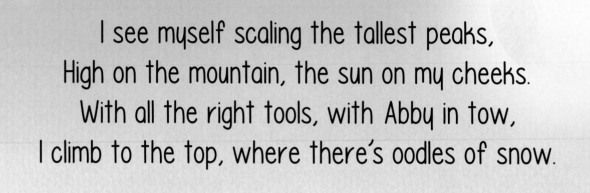

I see myself scaling the tallest peaks,
High on the mountain, the sun on my cheeks.
With all the right tools, with Abby in tow,
I climb to the top, where there's oodles of snow.

"Don't climb too high," says Dad. "You might get hurt."
"I'm afraid you'll fall down and land in the dirt."
I've fallen a few times . . . or maybe nine.
Falls happen a lot; I know I'll be fine.

For our next adventure, we're off to the beach.
I hope we see baby whales that jump and breach!

There's lots to discover in the deep blue sea.
Will I find a mermaid who looks just like me?

The water is shallow where I swim and splash.
My brothers go where the waves tumble and crash.

Mom says, "Stay on the beach. Play with your toys."
But I'm determined to be with the boys.

"See it, then be it," I always say.
If I believe I can, I'm nearly halfway.

I see myself with the wind whipping my hair,
Riding waves as sailfish soar through the air.
I'm surfing waves with Abby by my side,
Speeding past my brothers — a fantastic ride!

I'm sad that our adventures are almost done.
Let's head to the forest for a little more fun.

In the woods, animals play hide-and-seek.
My brothers and I swing high over the creek.

I've never made it to the swing on my own.
Today, I'm DETERMINED to do it alone.
Unsteady and nervous, I stumble and trip.
As I walk down the bank, I begin to slip.

I almost give up, but I stop, and I say,
"See it, then be it. I'm nearly halfway!"

Abby keeps me steady. I walk down the slope.
I reach for the swing and hold tight to the rope.

"Hooray, I did it!" I yell, feeling proud.
I never gave up. Now I'm touching a cloud!

Obstacles could stand in mine and Abby's way.
But that won't keep us from adventures each day.
"See it, then be it." Believe that it's true!
When I believe, there's so much more I can do.

We want you to know that you CAN do it too.
We're all MIGHTY inside. Yes, even you.

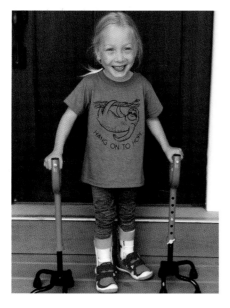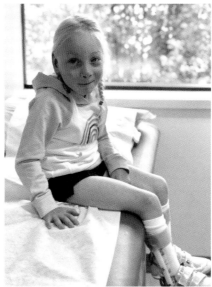

THE REAL-LIFE MIGHTY MISS MAYA & ABBY THE GOLDENDOODLE

What is Maya's diagnosis?
Maya has cerebral palsy, or CP for short. People with CP have trouble controlling their muscles. CP affects everyone differently. You can't catch CP. Usually a person is born with it.

Why does Maya use a walker, canes, and sometimes no devices in the story?
A person living with a disability might use more than one device to get around. People tend to think that because someone uses a walker or wheelchair, they can't walk independently. That's not true. A person with a disability might use a wheelchair, a walker, or canes when tired or have a long distance to travel, but ALSO walk on their own, just like Maya.

What are those things on Maya's legs called?
The things on Maya's legs are called Ankle Foot Orthotics or AFO's, but Maya just calls them her braces. They help make her legs strong, making it easier for her to walk.

How can I help someone with CP?
Be a good friend! Kids with CP like to play games, read, go to the beach, and do all the same things that you like. Being a good friend and including everybody are the best ways to help a person with CP.

FOR MORE ADVENTURES FOLLOW US!

on Instagram: @mightymissmaya
or Facebook: @beemightymissmaya

Why does Abby only have three paws?

She was born that way.

Why Mighty Miss Maya?

Most babies are born at 40 weeks and weigh about seven pounds. Maya was born at 26 weeks, weighing 1 lb. 10 oz. Babies born early are called preemies. Maya was a feisty preemie; she kept her nurses on their toes. They always used to say, "She's tiny but mighty." Pretty soon, everyone started calling her Mighty Miss Maya!

THE BEE MIGHTY TEAM

Jackson T., Weston T., Nana & Papa Wilton, Conner Saunders, Winston Fish, Mirabelle S.,
The Simons Family, Ms. Anna, Eli & Lucas, MK Weber, The Diabetic Mommies, The Werner Family,
The Widing Family, The Nogoski/Olrich Family, Judi Maloney, The Ashton Jojo Memorial Fund,
Adam, Marika & Tripp BeVier, Libby Struik, Maureen & Chris Harrington, Ivy The Very Determined Dog,
Stephanie, Chris, Sophie & Phoebe Jackson, Winter The Dolphin, The Kyser Family, The Bageris Family,
Finley Smallwood, Napa Boston PT Team, LBB Team, Lisa Heiser-Polin, Justin Polin, Oliva & Benjamin Polin,
Jan Palkowski, Jim Perkins, Bennett Kester, Kaleena Goodman, Galway Galaxy Fineberg - our 4 legged
baby girl, Stacy, Landry & Maisie Gilroy, Betsy Gibbs, Charlie & Christian Smith, The Stoltz-Guevara Family,
Janet Farinha, In memory of Lori Tallerico, Jenn Pflug Stevens, Gilberto Cisneros, Lexi, Riley, Noah & Julia,
Courtney, Kooper, David, Carter, Emma, Wyatt, Kristen, Noah R. & Aiden, Parker, Maddie, Izzy,
Ben & Nate, The Sluis Family, L.T. Arnold, Dr. Kirsten Wilhelm, Sara Vaughn, Mike Sluz, Hazel & Henry Cate,
Stacie Murley, Lauren & Sam DeHaan, Anthony, Renecca, Troi, Layna, Ashlyn, Connor, Nyla,
The Wooten Family, Sara, Brian & Finn Klebba, Jordy & Mayes, Griffin V.,
Ryan & Jenny Kehoe, Eleanor Rodríguez de Rubio Velázquez,
Nolan Moore, Kathy Gardner, Alex Green, Missy Gaisford,
Stevie & Stella, Rivka, Jocelyn Davis, Pamela Wood, Margaret
Croom, The Kessinger Family, Jack Sharpe, Kerry Philley,
The Sperry family, Christine Civick, Whitney Sanson Sherman,
Mickey Young, Crystal Molina, Dr. Park, Addison Dennis,
The Holm Family, Nikki Roberts, Grammy Beth & Papa Denny,
Molly, Mrs. Nelson & Bailey the Wonder Pup,
Smile Therapy For Kids, Elizabeth Ranzo, Dr. B., Zander,
Finn & Nora Johnson, The Moltzan Family, Jessica Lindberg,
Maya Cat, Grandpa Greg and Julie, Ryan Matura,
Ms. DeAnn, Josiah Gess and Family, The Kovacs Family,
Jay Miletsky, Dorthea, David Yates, Austin & Teddy,
Nathan, Cozi, & all our friends at Clearwater Marine Aquarium.